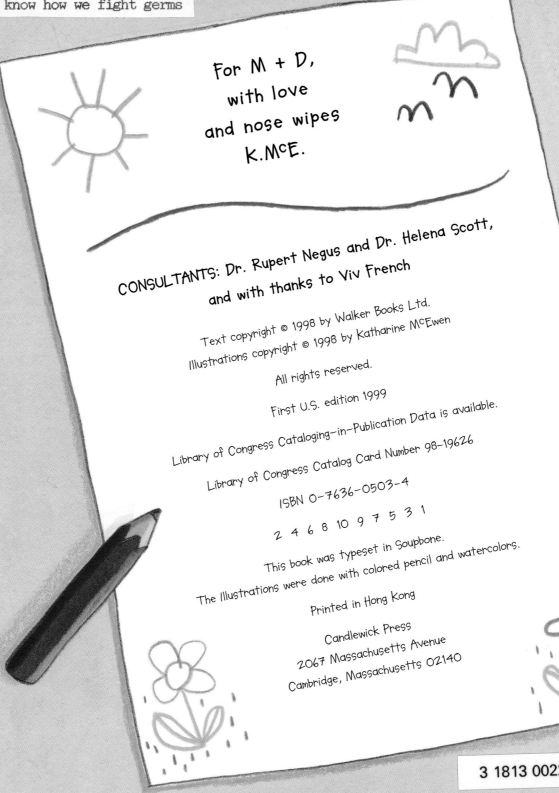

For M + D,
with love
and nose wipes
K.MᶜE.

CONSULTANTS: Dr. Rupert Negus and Dr. Helena Scott,
and with thanks to Viv French

Text copyright © 1998 by Walker Books Ltd.

Illustrations copyright © 1998 by Katharine McEwen

First U.S. edition 1999

Library of Congress Cataloging-in-Publication Data is available.

Library of Congress Catalog Card Number 98-19626

ISBN 0-7636-0503-4

2 4 6 8 10 9 7 5 3 1

This book was typeset in Soupbone.
The Illustrations were done with colored pencil and watercolors.

Printed in Hong Kong

Candlewick Press
2067 Massachusetts Avenue
Cambridge, Massachusetts 02140

I KNOW HOW WE FIGHT GERMS

KATE ROWAN

illustrated by

KATHARINE MᶜEWEN

CANDLEWICK PRESS
CAMBRIDGE, MASSACHUSETTS

"ATCHOOOOOO!"
Sam sneezed
a huge sneeze.

6

"Sam!" said Mom.
"That's GROSS!
 Don't you have a tissue?"
 And she pulled one out of her
 pocket and wiped his nose.

"Thanks," said Sam, and
 he sneezed again—
"ATCHOOOOO!"

"You have a cold,"
 said Mom.

"I know," said Sam, "and I know why colds make me sneeze. When I sneeze, I'm blowing cold germs out of my body."

sneeze

"You certainly are," said Mom. "That's how cold germs spread to other people, and why you need to catch your sneeze in a tissue. If someone else breathes in your cold germs, they might get a cold, too."

"Oh," said Sam.
"Is that how
I got this cold?"

"Probably," said Mom.
"I suppose you caught
it from someone at school."

ATCHOOO!

"We studied germs at school," said Sam. "My teacher said you can sneeze them a really long way. She said you can sneeze them as far as 10 yards."

"That IS a long way," said Mom.

"That's as far as three elephants standing in a line!"

Sam giggled. "I wouldn't like to be near an elephant when it sneezed!"

"ATCHOOOOO!"
Sam peered
at his tissue
"You can't see
germs, can you?"

"No," said Mom, "they're too tiny. Even the biggest ones are so small you could fit hundreds of thousands of them on the tip of your thumb. You can only see germs if you look at them under a microscope."

microscope

Sam sniffed.
"I bet I've got MILLIONS of germs inside me."

"BILLIONS!" said Mom. "But not all germs make us sick, and when they do, our bodies try to fight them off."

"I know," said Sam.

"I've got something in
my blood that fights germs."

water + red blood cells + white blood cells + platelets = blood

"That's right," said Mom.
"About half your blood is water,
but there are also lots of things
in it called **cells**—red ones and
white ones. And there are parts
of **cells** called **platelets**, too."

"There are?" asked Sam.
"Is that why blood is
red—'cause of
the **red blood cells**?"

Mom nodded.
"And the **white blood cells**
are the ones that kill the germs.
They make special chemicals.
Then they zap the cold
germs with the chemicals
and kill them."

"Cool," said Sam.

"Germ busters to the rescue!"

And he sneezed again.

chickenpox germ

"You should put your coat on," said Mom. "Keeping warm helps your body fight colds."

"Okay," said Sam. "But cold germs aren't the only bad germs, are they? 'Cause when I had chickenpox the doctor said I'd caught chickenpox germs."

"Yes, he did," said Mom.
"That's because there are lots of
different germs. They all do different
things, and scientists divide them
into groups. One group is
called **viruses**—cold germs
and chickenpox germs
are both **viruses**."

19

"Oh yeah, I remember," said Sam. "There are some germs called bac...something, too."

"Bacteria," said Mom. "They're another germ group. **Bacteria** live on all kinds of things, but they especially love dirt. So if you eat dirty food or don't wash your hands before meals, bad **bacteria** can get into your body."

Sam wiped his nose. "Do **white blood cells** zap the bac things, too?"

"They do kill them, but not by zapping," said Mom.

"When bad **bacteria** get into your blood, the **white blood cells** come along and gobble them up!"

"YUCK!" said Sam.

"Germ munchers to the rescue!"

21

"How do you know about **bacteria** anyway?" asked Mom.

Sam showed her the scab on his elbow.
"When I fell down at school, my teacher washed the dirt off and sprayed some stingy stuff on the cut. She said it was for the bac things."

"**Bacteria**," said Mom.

"Yeah," said Sam. "She said they might get into the cut. The spray helps to kill them, and then a scab grows to keep them out. She said scabs are made when blood gets all sticky and hard."

"That's where the **platelets** come in," explained Mom, "the parts of **cells** I was telling you about. Scabs are made by billions of **platelets** and **red blood cells** clumping and lumping together."

23

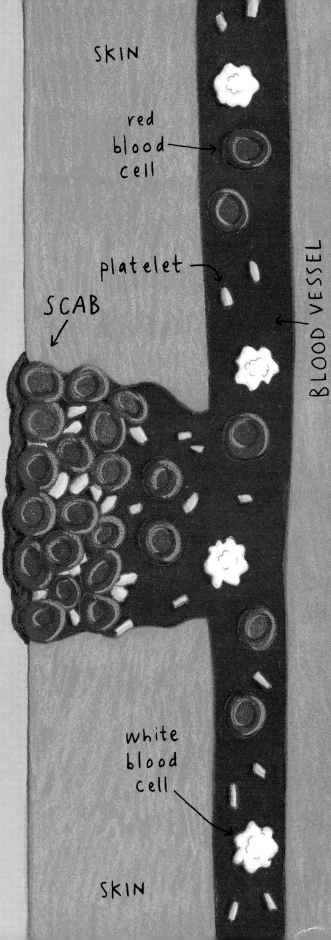

SKIN

red blood cell

platelet

SCAB

BLOOD VESSEL

white blood cell

SKIN

"Yeah," said Sam.
"And when the skin's healed,
the scab falls off."

"And that's why you need to keep
cuts clean and not pick at scabs
before they're ready to come
off by themselves," said Mom,
"so the bad **bacteria**
don't get in."

"I know," said Sam.
"But I LIKE picking
at scabs."

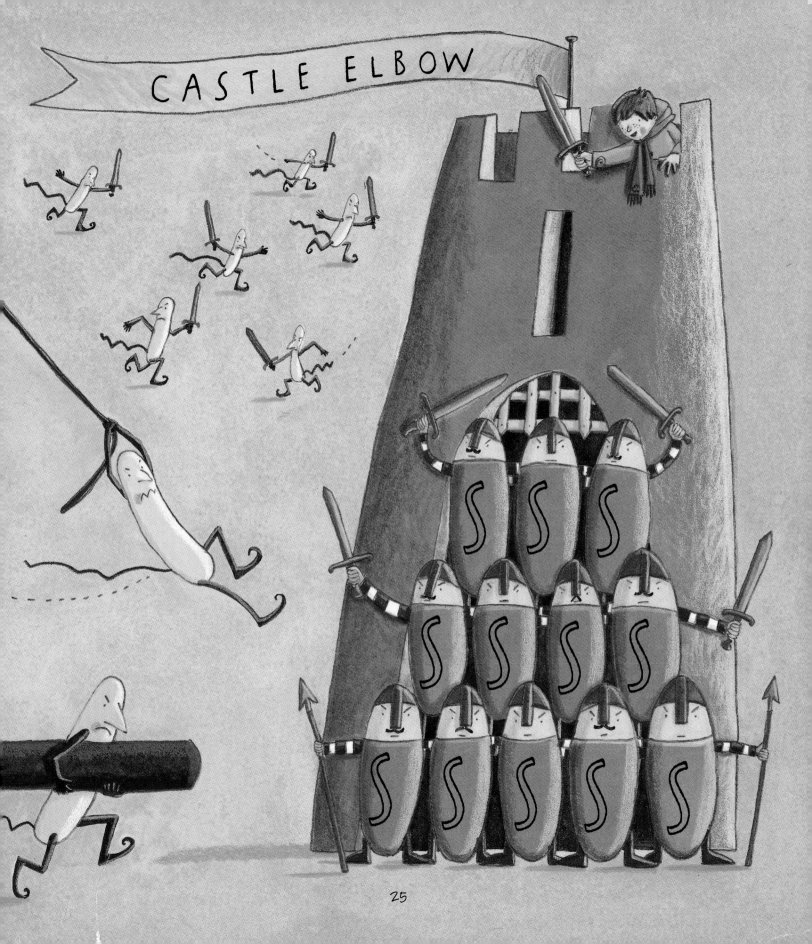

"Not all **bacteria** are bad, though," said Mom. "You have good **bacteria** living inside you all the time, helping to keep you healthy. And some food has good **bacteria** in it, too—like yogurt and cheese. There are even **bacteria** that help to make good soil."

"Do we have good soil?" asked Sam.

"Yes," said Mom. "That's why we grow such great vegetables!"

Sam sighed.

"Like spinach, you mean."

She sneezed a huge sneeze.

"Mom!" said Sam.

"That's GROSS!

Don't you have a tissue?"